SAM G

Tl
Headmaster's
Ghost

Illustrated by Gillian Hunt

HODDER
Wayland

an imprint of Hodder Children's Books

Chapter One

"Mortimer Hall is haunted," said Adam from the back seat of the coach. He poked Danny in the shoulders making him wince.

"Don't!" said Danny. He was tired and hungry and the last thing he wanted was Adam Caine making fun of him. Adam was a bully, just like his friend Melissa Glass. And now they were going to be together for a whole week. Danny had been looking forward to the school trip, but now he wasn't so sure.

"Calm down, everyone," called Mrs Judd from the front of the coach, "I know it's been a long journey but we'll be there soon."

Danny looked out of the window, hoping
to catch a glimpse of Mortimer Hall. But
there was nothing out there to see. It was
the middle of winter and an evening mist
billowed around the bus, shutting out the
view.

"Did you see that?" said Ahmed, Danny's
best friend.

"Did I see what?" asked Danny.

"There was someone standing by the side of the road. A short figure in a black cloak."

"Don't you start," said Danny. He peered out of the windows again but all he could see was a row of gnarled trees, their branches poking out of the thick mist.

Adam grinned. "I told you there's something sinister about this place," he said. "It's full of blood-sucking ghosts."

Just then the coach turned left into a car park.

"We're here at last," said Mrs Judd, standing up. "Welcome to Mortimer Hall, everyone."

Chapter Two

That night, Danny lay on his bed in the boy's dormitory. The moon seemed to shine brighter here than at home. Its light filtered through the curtains, making the shadows seem darker than ever.

Suddenly there was a knock at the door. Danny jumped. "Who's that?" he called.

"It's Melissa and Jodie," said Adam, sitting up in the bed next to his. "We're going to have a midnight party."

"Party?" The other boys sat up too, grinning from ear to ear. Ahmed opened the door and Melissa tiptoed in, followed by Jodie.

"We brought crisps," said Jodie, "and chocolate biscuits."

"Great," said Adam, "I've got a bottle of orange squash." His round face looked deathly pale in the moonlight. Danny looked away.

"We got this, too," said Melissa, holding up a book.

"So," laughed Ahmed. "What's so special about that?"

Melissa set the book on her lap. "I found it in the library," she said. "It's got all sorts of information about Mortimer Hall in it, including lots of stuff about the ghost that Adam was talking about on the coach."

"Great," said Ahmed, "read it out."

"Yeah," said Adam, sneering at Danny with dark, blue lips, "give us the creeps."

"Wait a minute," said Melissa. She fished a torch out of the carrier bag and switched it on, shielding the glare with her hand.

"Here we are," she said. " *'Mortimer Hall was built in the 1850s for the Mortimer family. In late Victorian times it was bought by the Scholars' Society and turned into a boys' school. Nowadays it is owned by the local education authority and used by many schoolchildren as a base to study local areas of interest.'* "

"We know that already," grumbled Ahmed, "read the bit about the ghost."

Melissa turned the page, squinting in the faint light to see better. "This is it: '*The ghost that haunts Mortimer Hall is said to be that of Edward Bosworth, who was headmaster of the school at the turn of the century. Like most teachers of his time, Mr Bosworth believed in discipline and is said to have been fond of using his cane. One night he was marking papers when he accidentally knocked over a lamp on his desk. In an instant the office went up in smoke. Mr Bosworth died a terrible, painful death.*' "

"That's gross," Ahmed whispered, grinning from ear to ear. "Read it again."

"I haven't finished yet," said Melissa.

" '*The ghost of Mr Bosworth has been seen many times. It roams around Mortimer Hall, looking for disobedient pupils to cane.*' "

"I don't believe that!" said Danny.

"It's written here, in black and white," said Melissa.

Adam turned to Danny. "You like that, Danny boy?"

"It's not as scary as some of the books I've read," said Danny, boldly. "I'm thirsty. Is there any squash left?"

"No," said Ahmed. "But there's a water fountain up the corridor. I could do with another drink, too."

The two boys left the room, closing the door behind them. Adam turned to Melissa. "That was *brilliant*," he laughed.

"It did sound spooky, didn't it?" Melissa said proudly. "None of you could tell I'd made up the bit about the ghost."

"You mean that part of the story wasn't really in the book?" Jodie gasped.

Adam shook his head and laughed. "There was a Mr Bosworth who burnt to death," he said, "but there is no ghost in Mortimer Hall. Melissa made that up because we're going to play a trick on Danny tomorrow night."

Chapter Three

Melissa looked up from the game of Scrabble she was sharing with Jodie.

"Danny, would you do me a favour?" she asked. "Would you get me a drink from the machine outside the dining room. I'd go myself but I'm sure Jodie will cheat the moment my back is turned."

"All right," Danny said. He took Melissa's money and left the common-room. If he was nice, she might leave him alone.

The way to the dining room was along a corridor and across a large assembly hall. The corridor was dimly lit. Rows and rows of ancient pupils and teachers looked down at him from framed pictures on the wall. Danny wondered which one of them was the headteacher who had burnt to death.

He reached the end of a corridor and
turned right into the assembly hall. It was
quite dark in there. The only light came from
a small neon sign saying EXIT above a door
on the far wall. Danny fixed his sight on the
sign and started walking towards it. For a
moment, he had a horrible feeling that the
rows of wooden seats on either side of him
were filled with long-dead students, all sitting
there in absolute silence, staring at him.

Danny stopped walking and forced himself to look around. There was no one there, of course. No dead students, no teachers. Danny breathed a sigh of relief. He was close to the EXIT sign now. A few more seconds and he'd be out of this horrible dark room.

Just then he heard a creak, as if someone had settled in one of the chairs. Danny stopped dead in his tracks. "Is anyone there?" he called. There was no answer.

Relieved, Danny took another step towards the EXIT sign. Then he heard another noise. It sounded like someone trying desperately to breathe, someone choking to death in smoke fumes.

Mr Bosworth.

Danny saw a figure on the other side of the hall. It was tall and thin, with drooping shoulders. On its head was a mortar board with a burnt tassel hanging down one side.

Danny thought of bolting but his legs seemed to be welded to the floor. Then the figure turned its face towards him and he could see a pair of red, glowing eyes scanning the dark. Its tongue was lolling out of a burnt, lip-less mouth.

"Danny Griggs," it whispered, "have you been a naughty boy?"

Danny felt the dark rush in on him, choking him. He took a step backwards from the advancing figure. Then he screamed.

Chapter Four

"You two are wicked!" said Jodie. "The whole place is buzzing with the news of what you did to Danny last night."

Melissa giggled. "I wish I'd been there to see Danny's face when he met Adam. It must have been quite a sight."

"I can't believe he fell for it," said Adam. "My rubber mask wasn't *that* good."

"Where did you find the mortar board?" asked Jodie.

Adam laughed. "In a box, in Mr Bosworth's old office."

"Poor Danny," said Ahmed.

"Don't you spill the beans on us," Melissa warned him, "or you'll be next."

The door opened and Danny came in. For a moment the whole common-room went quiet. Then someone shouted, "Hey, Danny, have you seen any ghosts lately?"

That made Adam and Melissa laugh, but Danny ignored them and went straight over to Ahmed. "Do you want to go to the shop and buy some chocolate?" he asked.

Ahmed nodded.

"Watch out for the ghost," Adam said.

"You watch out," said Danny, "you might bump into him, too."

"I'm not afraid of ghosts," said Adam, "not like some."

"I'm not afraid of ghosts, either," said Danny.

"Oh, yes you are," Adam sneered.

Ahmed nudged Danny with his elbow. "Leave it, Dan," he whispered.

"I *won't* leave it," said Danny hotly. "I'm not a coward."

"OK, then," Adam said. "Prove it."

Danny stuck out his chin. "How?"

"Spend tonight in Mr Bosworth's old office, the one where he was burnt to death."

"If I do," said Danny. "you'll have to stop picking on me."

Adam held out his right hand. "Put it there, Danny boy. It's a deal."

Chapter Five

Danny looked around him, trying to see in the dim light cast by a naked bulb above his head. The old office was piled to the ceiling with cardboard boxes. Rows of wooden shelves lined the walls. They were crammed with broken pieces of equipment. Right in the middle of the room was a desk with clawed feet like those of a dragon.

Danny imagined the place would have been spotless in Mr Bosworth's time. The dragon's feet would have been polished with beeswax. The shelves would have been groaning with books. Pictures would have covered the walls and maybe a few shields won in sports contests against other schools.

But not now. Cobwebs hung like curtains over everything, wrapping the boxes and the old equipment in grey shrouds. Danny shivered. What had possessed him to take up Adam's dare? Last night he'd been terrified of the ghost and now, here he was, waiting for it to return.

Danny saw a window with dusty panes. He tried to open it but it was locked. Outside the moon shone on a vast lawn and, beyond it, the dormitories. The lights were still on.

A knock at the door made him jump.

"Who is it?" he called.

"It's Ahmed," replied a voice on the other side of the door. "Are you all right in there?"

"Just about," said Danny. "Hey, Adam didn't leave the key in the door, did he?"

"No," said Ahmed. "But don't worry. There's nothing to be scared of."

Danny put his ear to the door. "What do you mean?"

"Melissa made the whole thing up," whispered Ahmed. "And Adam dressed up as the ghost, to give you a fright. I wanted to tell you sooner but I didn't get the chance. Melissa watched me like a hawk all day."

Danny breathed a sigh of relief. So there was no ghost then. The horrific figure he'd seen in the hall was just Adam, up to his stupid old tricks.

"Be careful," said Ahmed. "I think he's coming back to give you another fright. I've got to get back now. Good luck."

Danny listened to Ahmed's footsteps receding down the corridor. Then he sat on a pile of old newspapers. The room didn't seem at all forbidding now that he knew Mr Bosworth's ghost didn't really exist. Danny looked at his watch. It was eleven.

It would be ages before they'd let him out. He didn't want to fall asleep in case Adam turned up again. I'll read a book, Danny thought. That will help pass the time.

He picked an old volume from one of the shelves and shook it. Dust rose around him in a cloud, making him sneeze. He looked at the title on the cover: *Samuel Hughes versus the Smugglers.* It was a Boy's Adventure, the sort Danny's grandfather read when he was a boy. He opened it and started reading...

Chapter Six

Danny looked up from his book. All around him, the cobwebs were trembling. He consulted his watch – midnight, the witching hour.

A wispy mist blew in through the cracks in the window pane, bringing with it a faint musty smell. Danny wished he'd brought a jumper with him.

It was getting cold and dark. He looked up
at the bulb. Its light seemed dim and very far
away. Perhaps it was going to pop.

"Who gave you permission to touch that?"

Danny jumped. "Adam? How did you get
in?" he asked.

"Answer me, when I speak to you!" said
the voice angrily. "Who gave you permission
to touch that book?"

Danny's mind raced. How had Adam got into the room? Perhaps, he'd dozed off when he was reading.

"You're Griggs, aren't you?" said the voice. "A new boy. I'm surprised at you, sneaking in here without permission, handling my personal possessions."

"Come off it, Adam," said Danny, standing up. "I know it's you. You might as well give up and go to bed. You won't scare me again."

There was silence for a few seconds. Then the voice spoke again. "Turn off the light, please."

"No," said Danny firmly. "I've had enough of this. I'm going to tell Mrs Judd."

"Turn off the light," the voice ordered again. It sounded grown-up now, and angry. Danny had to admit Adam was getting very good at his practical jokes.

Suddenly the bulb shattered, plunging the room into darkness.

"There," said the voice, satisfied.

Danny waited for his eyes to get used to the dark. A moment later he could make out the shape of a man standing in front of him. He was short and plump, with a black cape fastened around his shoulders. That's not Adam, Danny thought, his flesh beginning to creep.

"I am Edward Bosworth, Headmaster of Mortimer Hall, 1893–1902. What your friend Melissa said about me is true. I cannot abide bad behaviour. But what I really can't stand is bullies. They keep me from resting in peace." He frowned angrily.

"A long time ago," he continued, "I believed that caning was the best method of dealing with bad behaviour. But now I know a much more effective way. Your so-called friends are about to be taught a lesson they'll never forget."

"What are you going to do to them?" asked Danny.

The ghost chuckled, making a horrible rasping sound that made Danny think of creaking coffins. "*Haunt them*, of course."

He fished a key out of a desk drawer and
held it out towards Danny. "I believe you will
need this to get through the door, but don't
follow me. I must do this alone."

Danny took the key, noticing how cold
to the touch it was. The ghost turned and
walked effortlessly through the locked door.

Danny imagined it hurrying down the corridor, its cape billowing around it like an angry raincloud. He pictured it floating up the narrow stairs to surprise Adam or perhaps Melissa. Then the lights in the dormitory across the lawn went out and Danny heard one long, piercing scream…

DARE TO BE SCARED!

Are you brave enough to try more titles in the Tremors series? They're guaranteed to chill your spine...

Beware the Wicked Web by Anthony Masters
In the dead of night, Rob and Sam explore the forbidden attic at the top of their new home. When they find a sprawling, sticky web, with a giant egg at its centre, they are scared – but not nearly as scared as when they discover that the egg is just about to hatch...

The Curse of the Frozen Loch by Anthony Masters
Why does the ghostly figure skate the loch in the dead of night? And what is wrong with Great-Aunt Fiona? Will and Sarah are determined to solve the mystery and save Fiona. But will they be the next victims of the curse of the frozen loch?

The Root of Evil by Barbara Mitchelhill
When Jake, Amy and Wez find the old pocket watch, they are thrilled. "We'll sell it!" says Jake. After all, finders are keepers, aren't they? So they sell the watch and go on a wild spending spree. But then things go horribly and frighteningly wrong...

All these books and many more can be purchased from your local bookseller. For more information about Tremors, write to: The Sales Department, Hodder Children's Books, A division of Hodder Headline, 338 Euston Road, London NW1 3BH.